A Year with Friends

A Year with Friends

by John Seven   illustrated by Jana Christy

abrams appleseed   new york

Cataloging-in-Publication Data has been applied for
and may be obtained from the Library of Congress.
ISBN: 978-1-4197-0443-7

Text copyright © 2012 John Seven
Illustrations copyright © 2012 Jana Christy
Book design by Meagan Bennett

Abrams Appleseed is a trademark of Harry N. Abrams, Inc.

Printed and bound in China
10 9 8 7 6 5 4 3 2 1

For bulk discount inquiries, contact specialsales@abramsbooks.com.

ABRAMS

THE ART OF BOOKS SINCE 1949

115 West 18th Street
New York, NY 10011
www.abramsbooks.com

For our sons Harry and Hugo,
who make every year a new adventure

January

is time for rolling down hills.

February

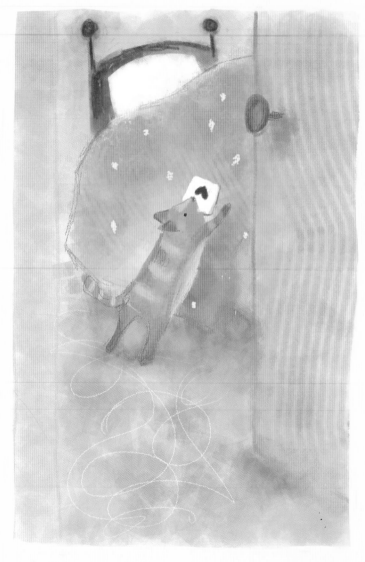

is time for snuggling.

March

is time to hold on to your hat.

April

is time to get messy.

May

is time for flowers.

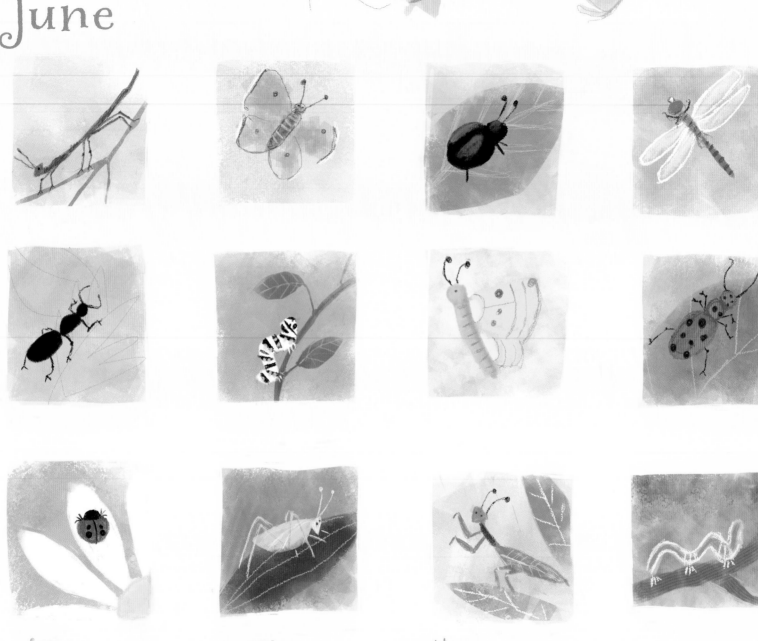

June

is time for bugs.

July

is time for fireworks.

August

is time for the beach.

September

is time for picking apples.

October

is time for tricks and treats.

is time to feast together.

December

is time for sharing.

A new year

is time for fun with new friends!